To my cuckoo banana students:
I love you all dearly and hope you remember to always believe in yourselves.

& to my own little cuckoo bananas: Lyelli and Noah. I love you so much! Thank you for inspiring me everyday.

The morning bell rings and what do we do to start the day?

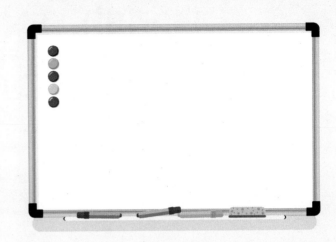

We wave, we tell jokes, we laugh, and **we play**! This class is cuck**oo** bananas!

It's time to read some books
and what do we do?

We lay on the floor and read with stuffed animals. It's true! This class is cuckoo bananas!

It's math time and **how will we** **review** t**o**da**y?**

We team up and play! We make basketballs
with our problems after we've solved them.
This class is cuckoo bananas!

It's time to walk in the halls. How do you think we will act?

We show ALL the other bananas **what to do. We have a big** impact. **This** class is cuck**oo** bananas!

It's time for lunch. **Do yo**u know what **we do** when **we're** hun**gry?**

We grab our food quickly,
before you start to hear our
tummies. This class is cuckoo
bananas!

It's time **for re**cess. **Do yo**u want t**o** kn**ow so**m**e**thin**g** nutt**y**?

Sometimes when we play outside we can get super muddy! This class is cuckoo bananas!

It's time to write. Do you think there is only one way?

We use white boards, and **pos**ters, and ma**gn**ets, and **s**and trays. This class is cuck**oo** bananas!

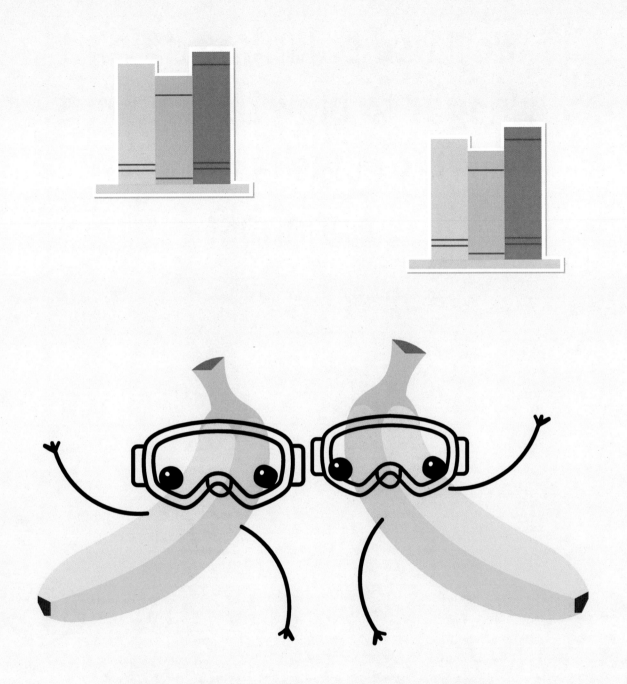

It's time **for** science and what will **we** do?

We'll use baking soda and vinegar to blow up balloons. This class is cuckoo bananas!

It's the end of the day. Do you know what comes next?

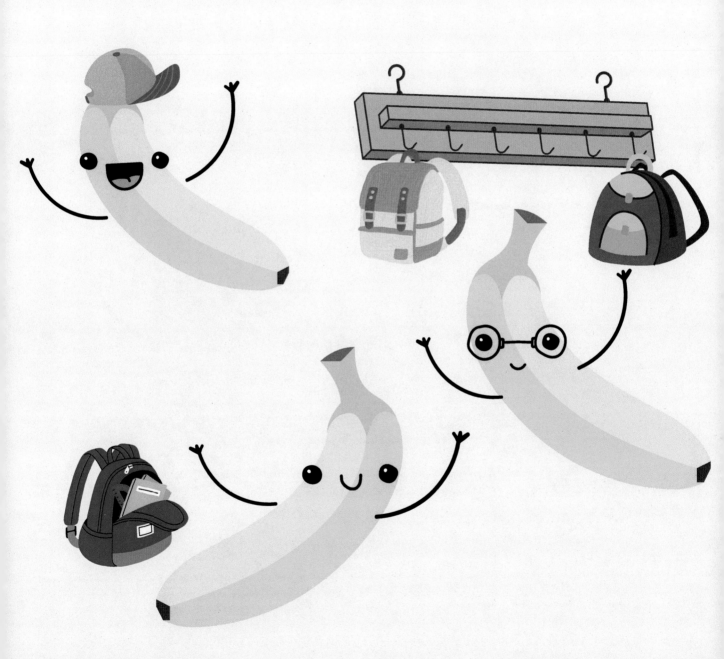

We all come together to sit and reflect.

We share with each other a compliment or two from our exciting day of learning as most cuckoo bananas do.

You really tried your best today! Hip hip horray!

Every cla**ssroo**m **sho**uld **be** this fun, d**o**n't **bel**i**eve** me? **It's true!**

I think being cuckoo bananas is the best way to learn, don't you?

Made in the USA
Monee, IL
24 October 2022

16490868R00017